Ralmas Johnson

Russey

Annie

To Tyler & Bradleigh
  Follow your dreams & find
your treasure, whatever it
may be!

Annie Goes to Oak Island

by
Cyndi Bussey
and Raymond Johnson

Illustrated by
Carolyn Watson-Dubisch

A portion of the proceeds from the sale of this book
will be donated to IWK: https://iwkfoundation.org/

Published in 2019 by www.anniegoesto.com

ISBN: 978-0-578-48796-0

This book is dedicated to Drake Tester

Thanks to Izzy Sampson who inspires us!
Also thanks to the Oak Island Team, and a special thanks to Oak Island Tours,
for their help and support.

Annie the whippet can't wait until tomorrow!
Annie and her friend Izzy are going to go to Oak Island
to look for treasure! What an adventure to have
with a good friend! What will they find there?
Annie hopes the treasure is lots of dog bones to eat.
Annie goes to sleep with dog bones dancing in her head!

The next morning, Annie and Izzy go to the
Causeway road which leads to Oak Island. Izzy has a
treasure map, they look to see where they should go first.
The map says go see Dan Blankenship, who lives on the
island and who has hunted treasure here for over 50 years!

Annie and Izzy meet Dan, who's at the Oak Island Museum.

Annie barks at Dan, and Izzy says, "Hi Dan, Annie wants to know if you have her dog bones? She is looking for them everywhere, and she thinks they might be buried on the island."

Dan says, "Well, I have been searching this island for many years, and I have found a lot of treasure, but I have never found any dog bones. We have a great team of searchers, and there are many places to look. You should go to the Research Center. Maybe someone there will have an idea about finding your treasure."

Outside the research center, Annie and Izzy meet Craig Tester
and his two sons, Drake Tester and Jack Begley.
They are getting ready to start their treasure hunting today!

Craig sees Izzy and says, "Well hello, Izzy and Annie, nice to see you today!"
Izzy says, "Hi, everyone. What are you doing today?"
Drake says, "Izzy, my dad, my brother, and I are going to go treasure hunting.
We love working on the island together. We love being a family. For us, it is Forever Family!"
Izzy smiles and says, "It is so nice that you can spend time together hunting for treasure.
Annie and I are good friends, and we are looking for dog bones for Annie."
Jack laughs and says, "Annie and Izzy, you should go find Doug Crowell in the War Room.
He knows everything about the island!"

On the way to the war room, Annie and Izzy meet a chipmunk
living where the McGinnis house used to be. Daniel McGinnis was one
of the first people to search for treasure, hundreds of years ago!
Maybe they buried dog bones in the foundation of his house!
Annie barks at the chipmunk, and the chipmunk says,
"No, Annie and Izzy, no bones
here, only Oak Island acorns!"
Izzy says, "OK, we will try the war room next."

Annie and Izzy walk down to where Dan and Charles are at a big table with a wire screen in the bottom.

"What are you doing?" Izzy asks.

Dan says, "Charles and I have a very important job. Every bucket of dirt we dig up, which we call 'spoils,' has to be looked through very carefully, because we can find small things that are very old and are clues to who was here many years ago. We can get very dirty doing this, but we have so much fun!"

Izzy asks, "Have you found any dog bones in the things you have dug up?"

"No, Izzy," Charles says. "We have found pottery and leather and a special paper called parchment, but no dog bones. I would try the swamp. Marty and Tony are down there right now!"

They find Tony and Marty at the stinky swamp! Marty dislikes the swamp because it smells so much, but Tony loves diving in the icky, smelly water! Tony is in a dive suit in the water, and Marty is sitting in a little boat called a dinghy, with a clothespin on his nose!

Annie barks, and Izzy says, "You are treasure hunters; have you seen any dog bones in the swamp?"

Tony says, "I am not a treasure hunter; I'm a treasure finder! I have found really neat things in the swamp. There may even be a ship sunk in this water! But no dog bones."

Marty says, "Who would want to chew on smelly swamp water–covered dog bones anyway! I think you should go to the Money Pit. There are more treasure hunters there who can help you."

Annie and Izzy go to the famous Money Pit, where it is said a big treasure was buried hundreds of years ago. People have dug many holes in the ground over hundreds of years, looking for the treasure that is said to be buried here. Annie sees Dave and Alex at the big hole in the ground called 10x.

Izzy says, "Dave, what is in this big hole?"

"Well Izzy." Dave says, "my father, Dan and I have been digging in this spot for many years, and we have dug a hole almost 200 feet deep! But it keeps filling with water so we have not been able to get to the bottom to see."

Rick is nearby planting flowers in a beautiful flower garden.
Izzy asks, "Rick, why are you planting flowers here?"

Rick says, "Well, Izzy, there have been many men throughout the years
who have searched here, and their wives and mothers have been here for them,
helping them in their quests, but they have never been thanked. So, this
is a garden to say thanks to all of the women who have helped the quest over the years."

Annie and Izzy continue down the hill and find Gary with his metal detector looking for treasure in Smith's Cove. Peter is there too, with a shovel, ready to dig up anything that Gary can find with his detector.

Annie barks, and Gary says, "Well, hello, little whippet, and hello, Izzy!"
Izzy asks, "What are you doing?"
Peter replies, "We are looking for treasure on this beach, and we are looking for tunnels that might go back up to the Money Pit."
Izzy says, "Annie and I are on a treasure hunt to find dog bones; have you found any?"
Gary says, "When I find a great treasure—what I call a bobby dazzler—I always say, 'Holy Shamoly' and put the treasure in my top pocket. I'm sorry there are no dog bones in my top pocket. But, I think Cindy and Lisa at the museum may know where to find some for you."

Annie and Izzy go to the open grassy area and
they see big X on the ground! X marks the spot!
On top of the X there is a dog bowl
FULL of dog bones! Wow!
They found their treasure!

As Annie and Izzy leave the island, with a big dog bone in Annie's mouth,
Izzy says "Annie, I think the best part of our treasure hunt was being together,
friends are the BEST kind of treasure!" Annie wags her tail and barks!

What kind of treasure would you look for?
Find a friend and go searching! Good luck in your quest!